God is Good

The Squirrel

and

the Nut

By Mrs. James Swartzentruber

Pictures by Lester Miller

To the Teacher:

This book is designed to give constructive reading practice to pupils using the grade one *Bible Nurture and Reader Series*. It uses words that have been introduced in the reader or can be mastered with phonics skills taught by Unit 3, Lesson 5. A few new words also appear in the story, printed in italics. At the end of the book, these words are listed with pronunciations and / or illustrations to help the children to learn them on their own. Be sure the children understand that the words are vocabulary or sound words except the words in italics, and where to look to learn new words if they need help. They should be able to read this book independently.

Books in this series with their placement according to reading and phonics lessons:

Copyright, 1989

By

Rod and Staff Publishers, Inc.
Crockett, Kentucky 41413
Telephone (606) 522-4348

Printed in U.S.A.

ISBN 978-07399-0058-1

Catalog no. 2249

"Here I come!" And Ray jumped right into a big pile of leaves!

Jean came next. She jumped
into the leaves too.

Again and again the children
jumped. Soon the leaves were not
on a nice, big pile.

"Ray, let's rake the leaves into a pile again," called Jean.

Ray and Jean raked the leaves into a nice, big pile again. There are so many leaves!

Jean stopped. There was a by the large oak tree. "See, Ray," she said.

Jean and Ray saw the . They saw the pick up a nut and run.

"What is he doing?" asked Ray.

The  ran near the sand box. He put the nut into the ground and covered it. Then he ran back to the oak tree. Again he picked up a nut. This time he ran to *another place.* Again he covered the nut.

Again and again the  got a nut and covered it.

"What are you doing,  ?" called Ray.

Away ran the  ! He ran up the tree and sat where he could see the children. He felt safe up there.

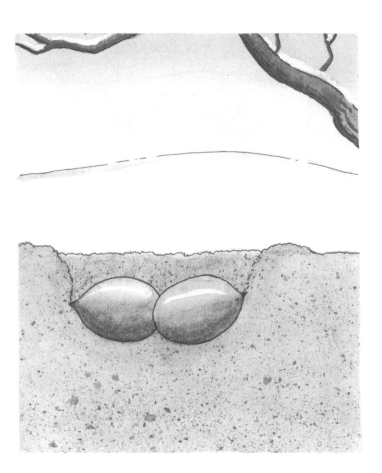

After many days it was cold.
The children did not play in the
leaves any more. Snow covered
the ground. The nuts were still
just where the 🐿️ hid them.

Sometimes Ray and Jean played with the sleds. What fun it was to zoom down the hill on the sleds!

Jean and Ray made a *snowman*. As long as it was cold, the *snowman* stood there. Did he stand very long when it was not cold? No, he melted and melted.

Then he was not a *snowman* at all . . .

. . . He was just water!

One day Jean was standing at the window. A  was running on the snow. He stopped and dug in the snow. Up he came with a nut!

"Mother! Ray!" Jean called,
"Come see what I see."

Mother and Ray came. The
 went to *another* spot.
Again he dug in the snow, and
again he came up with a nut!

"How can he find the nuts?" asked Jean. "How does he know where they are?"

Mother said, "When the nuts fell from the tree, the hid them in the ground. Now it is food for him when it is cold."

"But how can he remember where he hid them?" asked Jean.

"God helps the to know that," said Mother. "He made the that way so that he can get food when it is cold. God has a plan for all the animals. This is His plan for the .

"Now I remember!" cried Jean. "Remember, Ray, when he hid them while we were playing in the leaves?"

"Yes! Yes!" Ray remembered. "We did see him hide nuts! We save food for when it is cold too," he said. "But we do not hide it!"

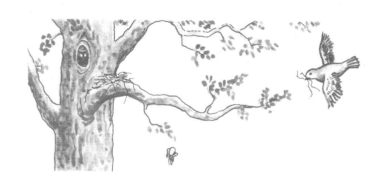

When spring came, it was not cold. The children did not play in the snow. There was no snow on the ground. Leaves were on the trees again. The grass was nice and green. The children liked to run 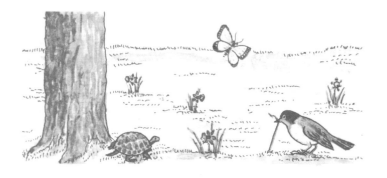 on the grass.

Then one day Ray found
something. "Jean, what is this?"
It was a plant in the grass, but
it was not grass.

"Mother," called Ray to
Mother who was *nearby*. "What
is this plant?"

Mother came to see. She
smiled. "It is a little oak tree,"
she said. "Who planted it?"

"I did not," said Ray.

"I did not," said Jean.

23

"Think a little," Mother said with a smile. "I think you will know who planted it."

But Ray and Jean did not know who planted the little tree.

Then Jean remembered something! "The did!" she cried.

Ray smiled. He remembered too!

I think that is right." Mother smiled at the children. "The planted it. Who made it grow?"

"God did!" said Ray.

"Let's ask Father if we can let this tree grow. It is by the sand box. It would make nice shade there."

"Yes, I think it would be a nice *place* for a tree," said Father.

When it was cold, the leaves fell. But after spring came again and it was warm, new leaves grew. The tree grew a little more.

Again it was cold, and the little oak tree had no leaves. Again spring came. The tree grew a little bigger.

The next *year* it grew a little
more . . .

. . . and the next year a little more.

Every year it grew a little
bigger.

Now the tree is a big tree. It makes lots of shade from the sun. Many birds have nests in the tree. hide nuts that fall from the tree for food when it is cold. A swing hangs from the tree. Children like to play on the swing.

But Ray and Jean do not play in the shade of the big oak tree. They sit and rest. Ray and Jean are not children. They are old. Ray has children, and his children have children. . . . Jean has children and her children have children. Their *grandchildren* now play in the shade of the big oak tree . . . that the planted . . . that God made to grow!

another (an + other)

place (plās)

snowman (snow + man)

nearby (near + by)

grandchildren (grand + children)

Key

year *near*—year